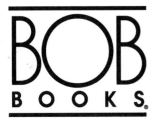

BOB BOOKS

SCHOLASTIC READER
LEVEL 1
50-250 WORDS

Cupcake Surprise!

by LYNN MASLEN KERTELL
illustrated by SUE HENDRA

SCHOLASTIC INC.

New York   Toronto   London   Auckland

Sydney   Mexico City   New Delhi   Hong Kong

ISBN 978-0-545-38269-4

Copyright © 2012 by Lynn Maslen Kertell. All rights reserved. Published by Scholastic Inc. by arrangement with Bob Books® New Initiatives LLC. SCHOLASTIC and associated logos are trademarks and/or registered trademarks of Scholastic Inc. BOB BOOKS and associated logos are trademarks and/or registered trademarks of Bob Books Publications LLC.
Lexile® is a registered trademark of MetaMetrics.

12 11 10 9 8 7 6 5 4 3 2 1   12 13 14 15 16/0

Printed in the U.S.A.   40
First printing, February 2012

It is Dad's birthday.

What will Jack and Anna
give to Dad?

Will they make a card?
Will they jot a note?
Will they sing a song?

Jack and Anna will
make cupcakes for Dad.

Cupcakes will be a big surprise.

Anna has the cookbook.

Jack gets eggs, sugar, and

There is no flour.

That is not a good surprise.

Jack and Anna go to the store.

At the store they get flour.
They get cookies, too.

Jack puts in flour and sugar.
Anna puts in milk, butter, and eggs.

Stir it up, Jack!

Uh-oh! The cookies fall in.
That is a surprise.

They mix in the cookies.

Oh, no! Chips fall in.
That is a surprise.

They mix in the chips.

Stir it all up, Jack.

Buddy wants to help, too.

Mom puts the cupcakes in to bake.

Jack and Anna watch the cupcakes.
Buddy watches, too.

The cupcakes look good.

Happy birthday, Dad!

Here are your birthday cupcakes.

Surprise!
These cupcakes taste great!